The G

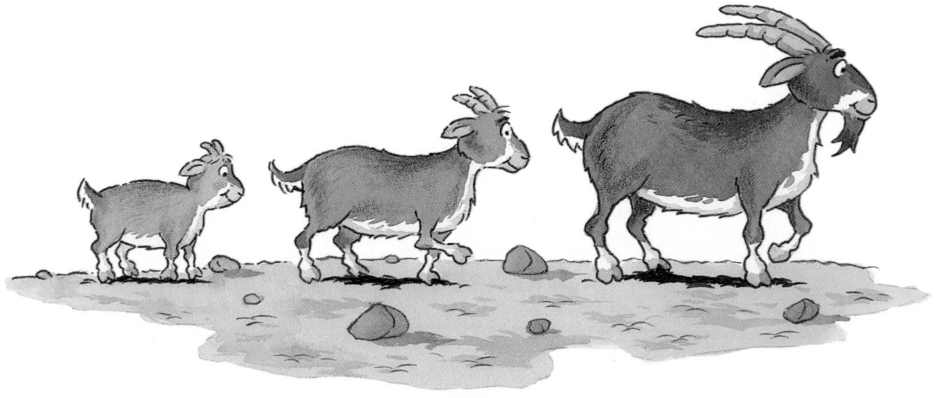

Illustrated by Richard Hoit

Rigby

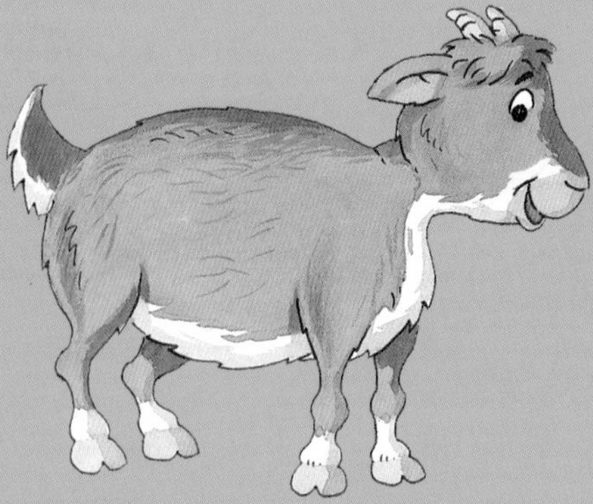

I am a goat.

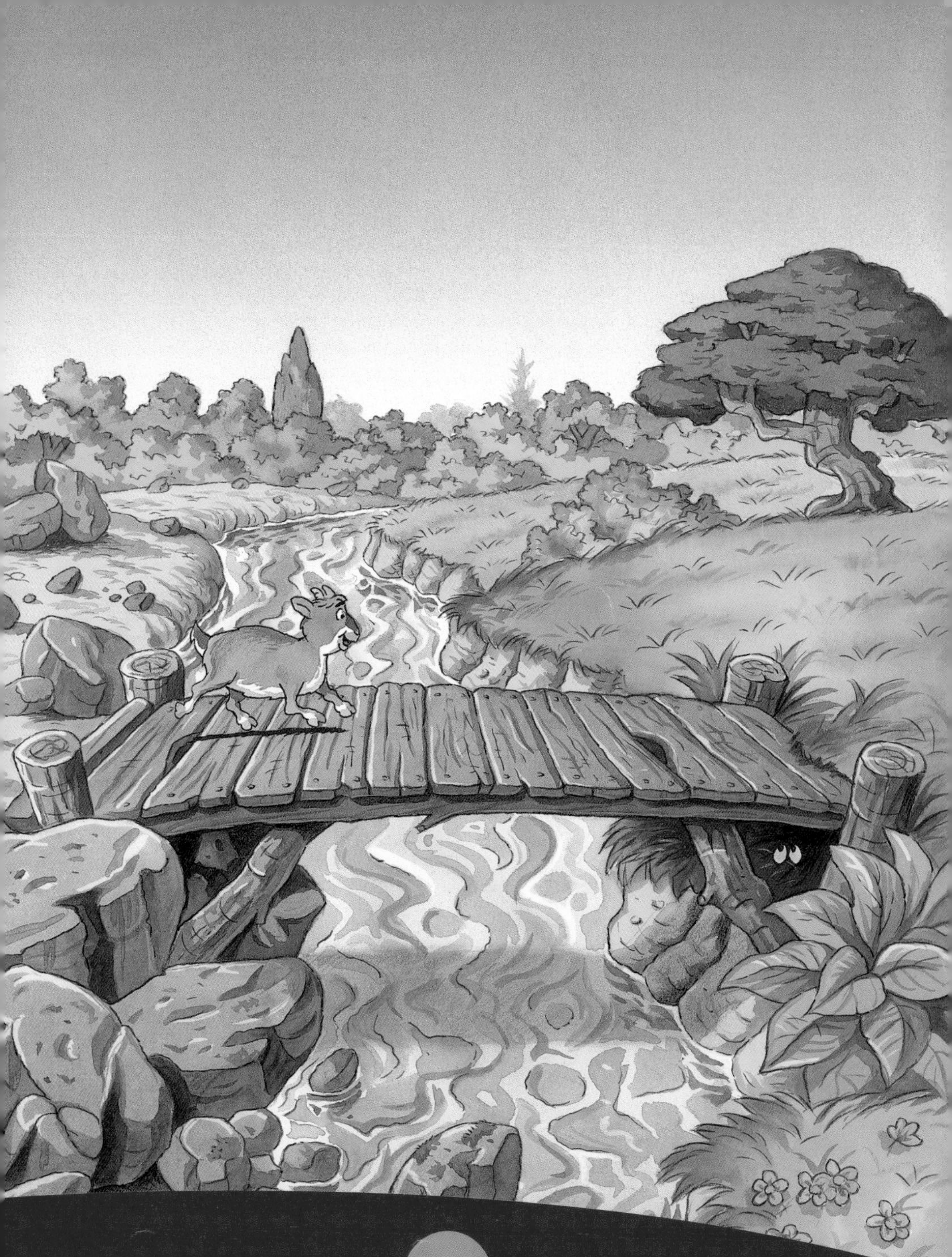

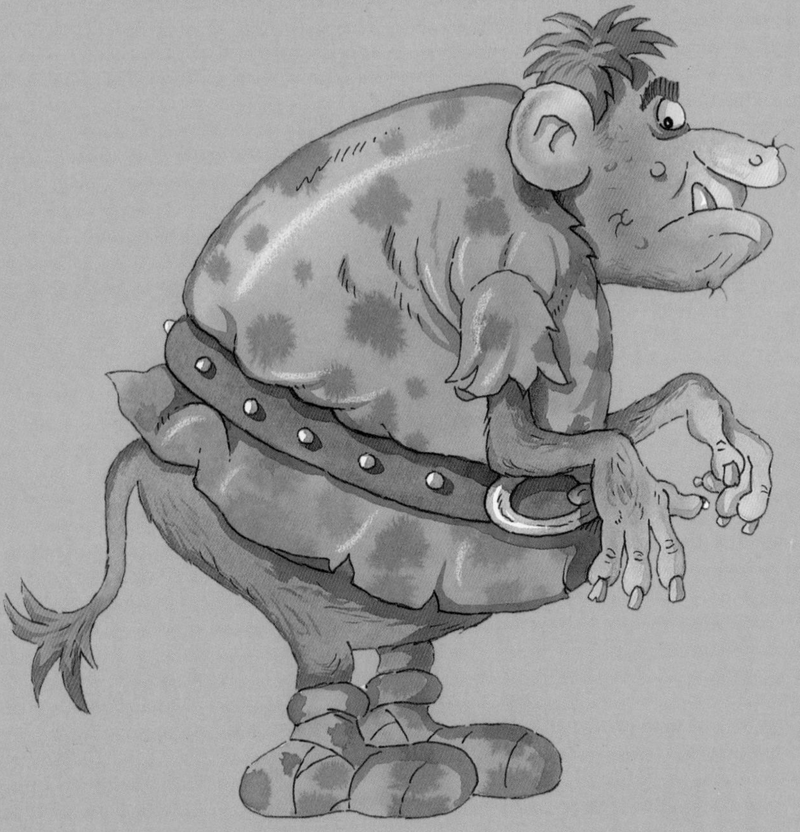

I am a monster.

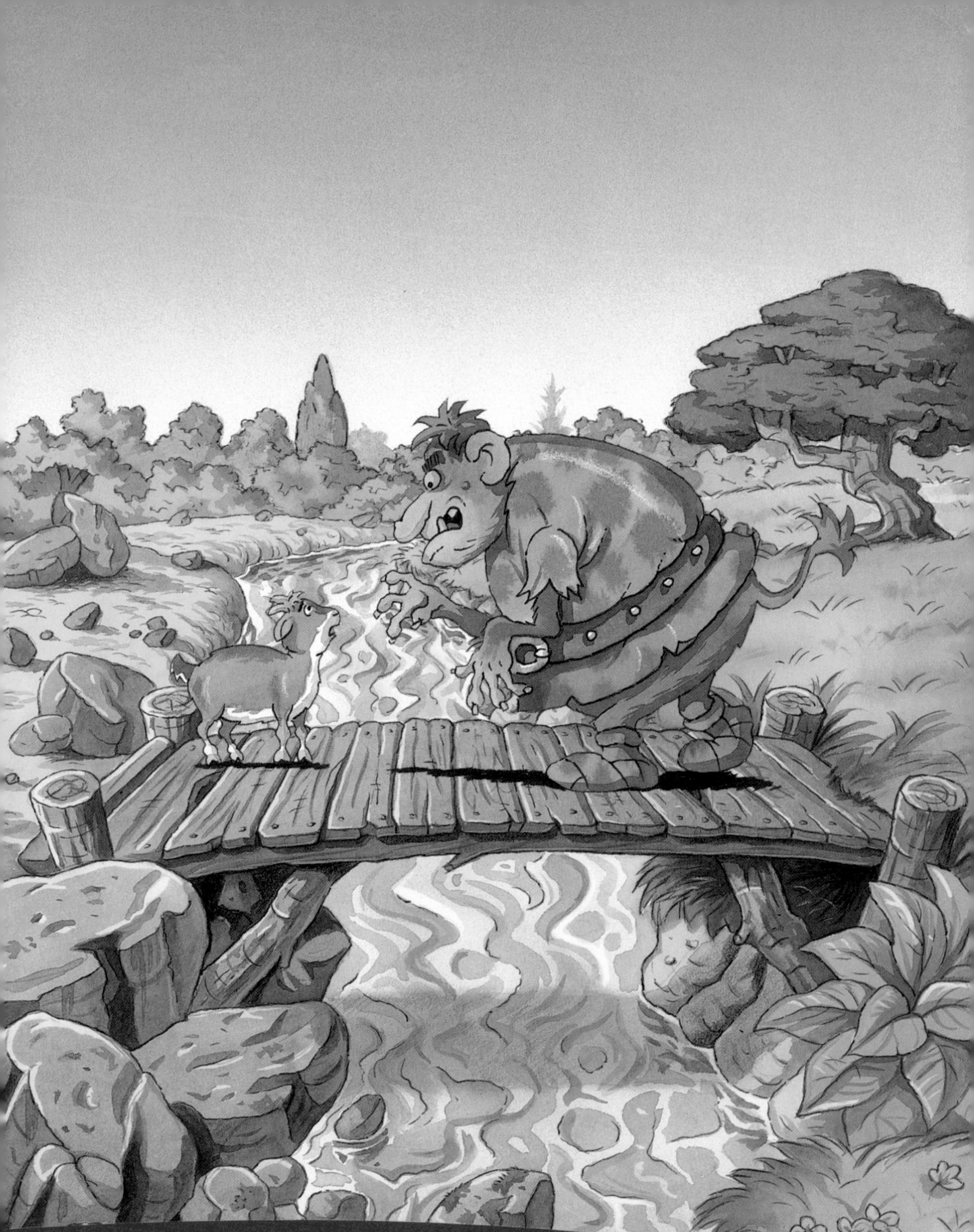

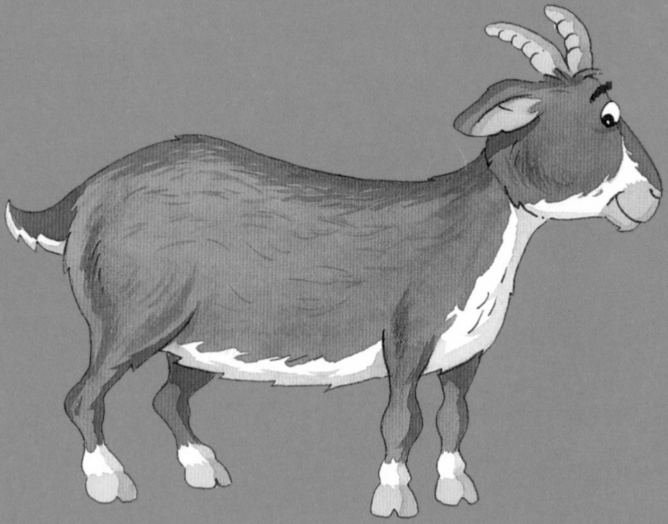

I am a goat.

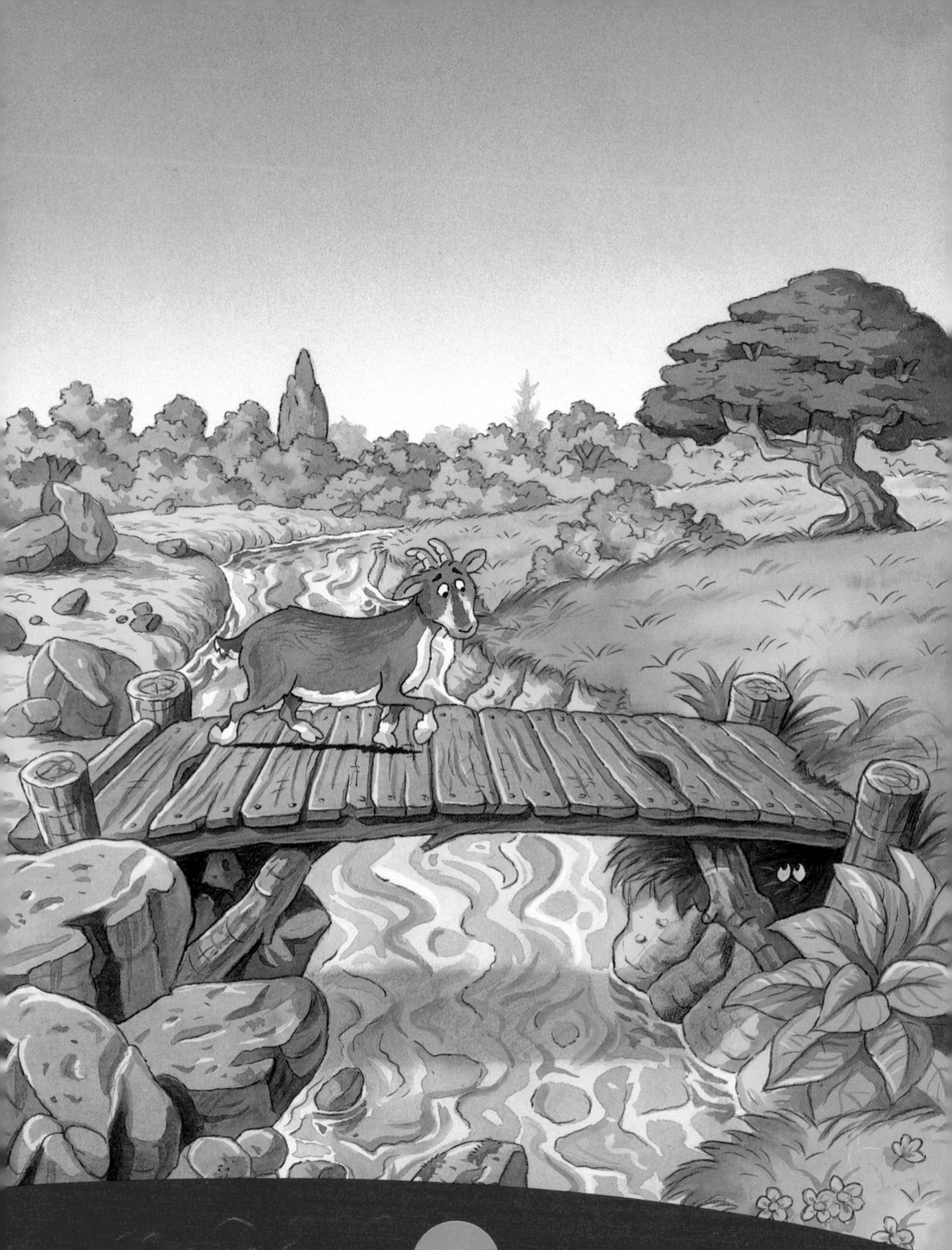

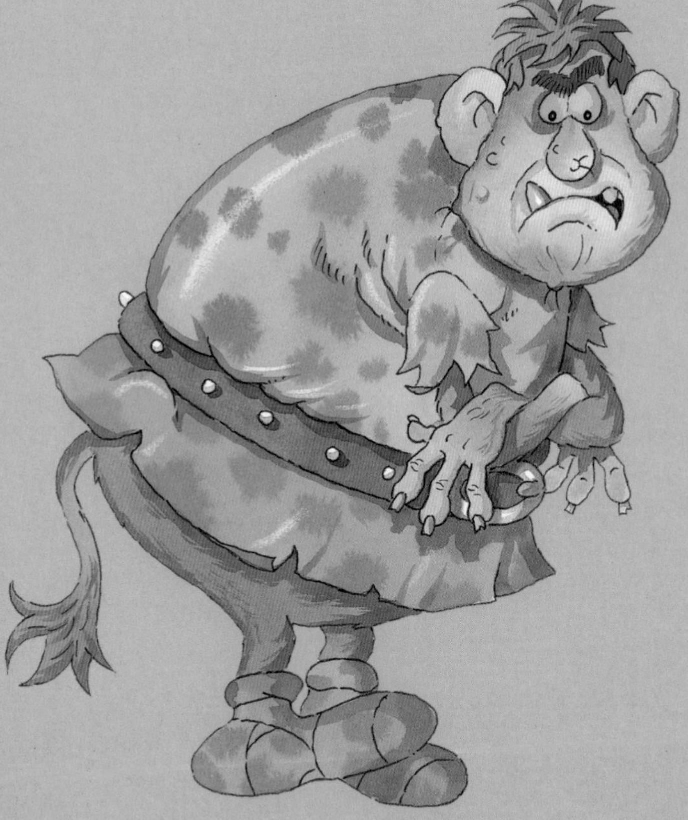

I am a monster.

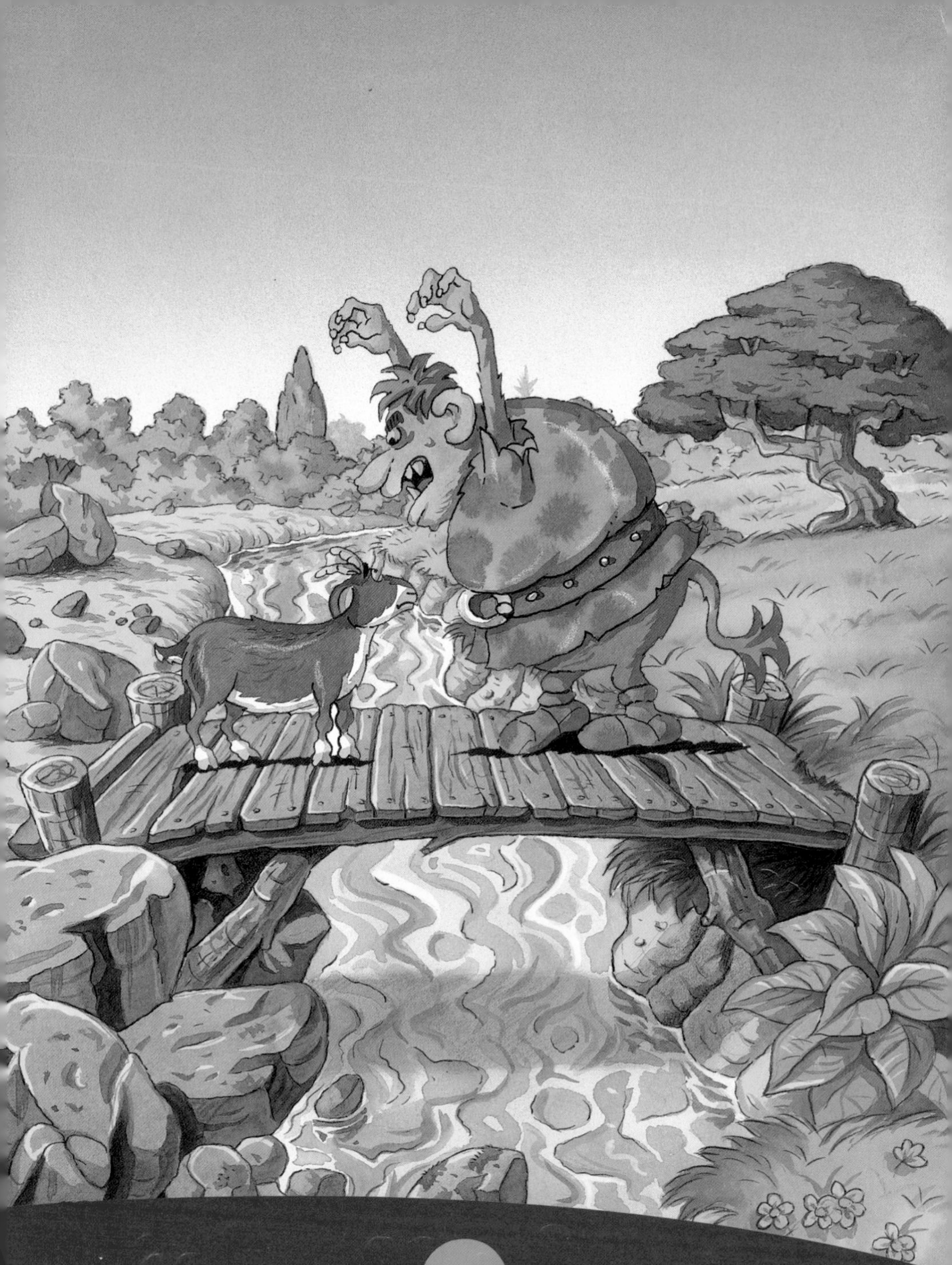

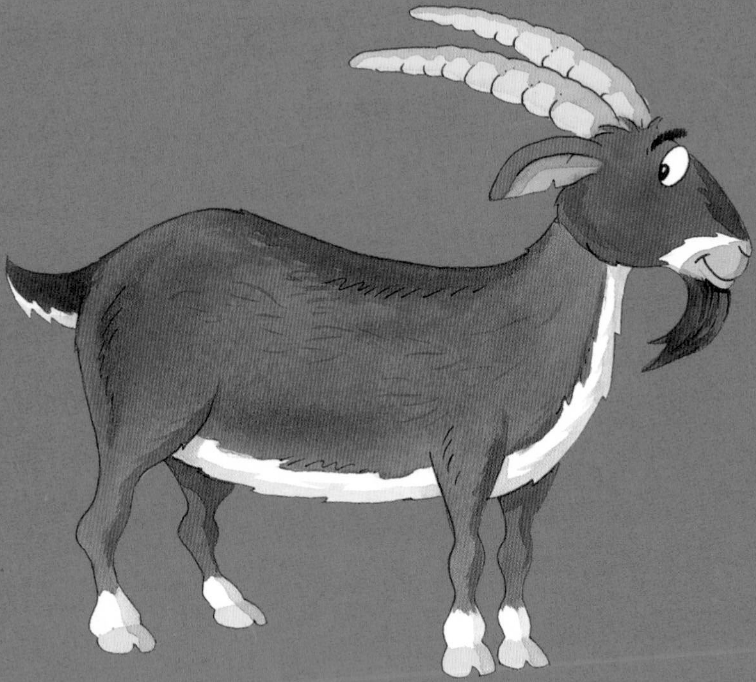

I am a goat.

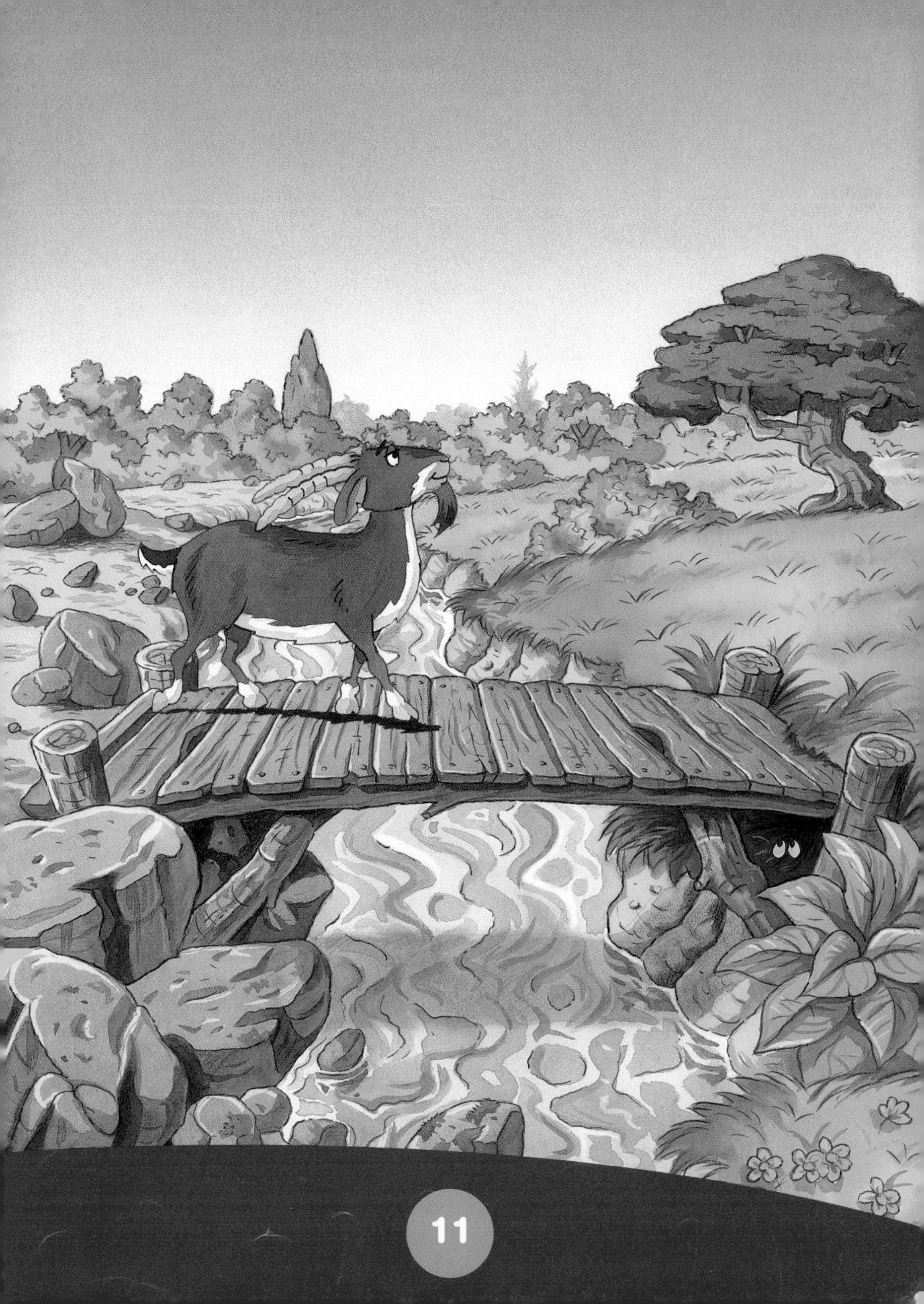

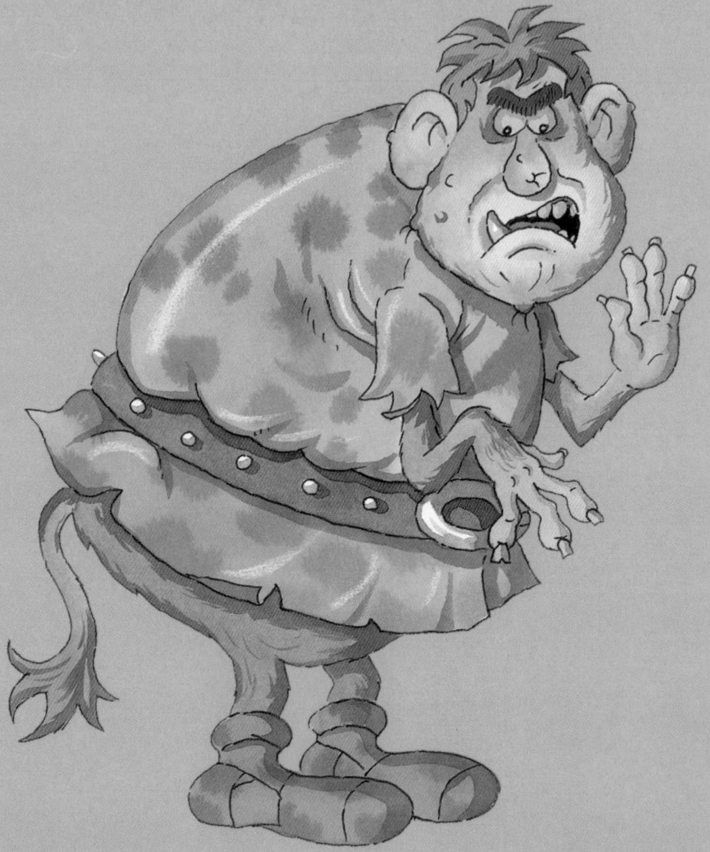

I am a monster.

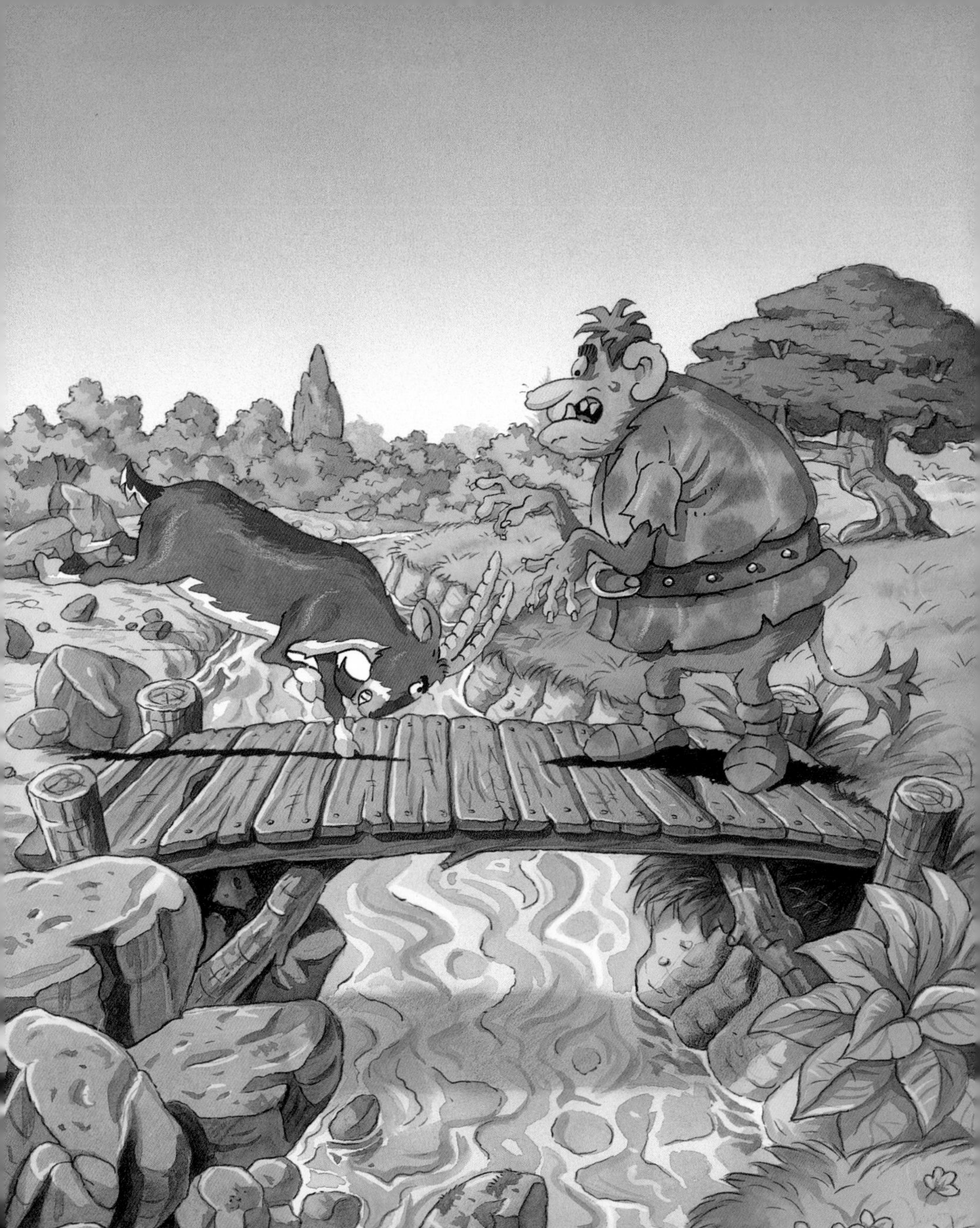

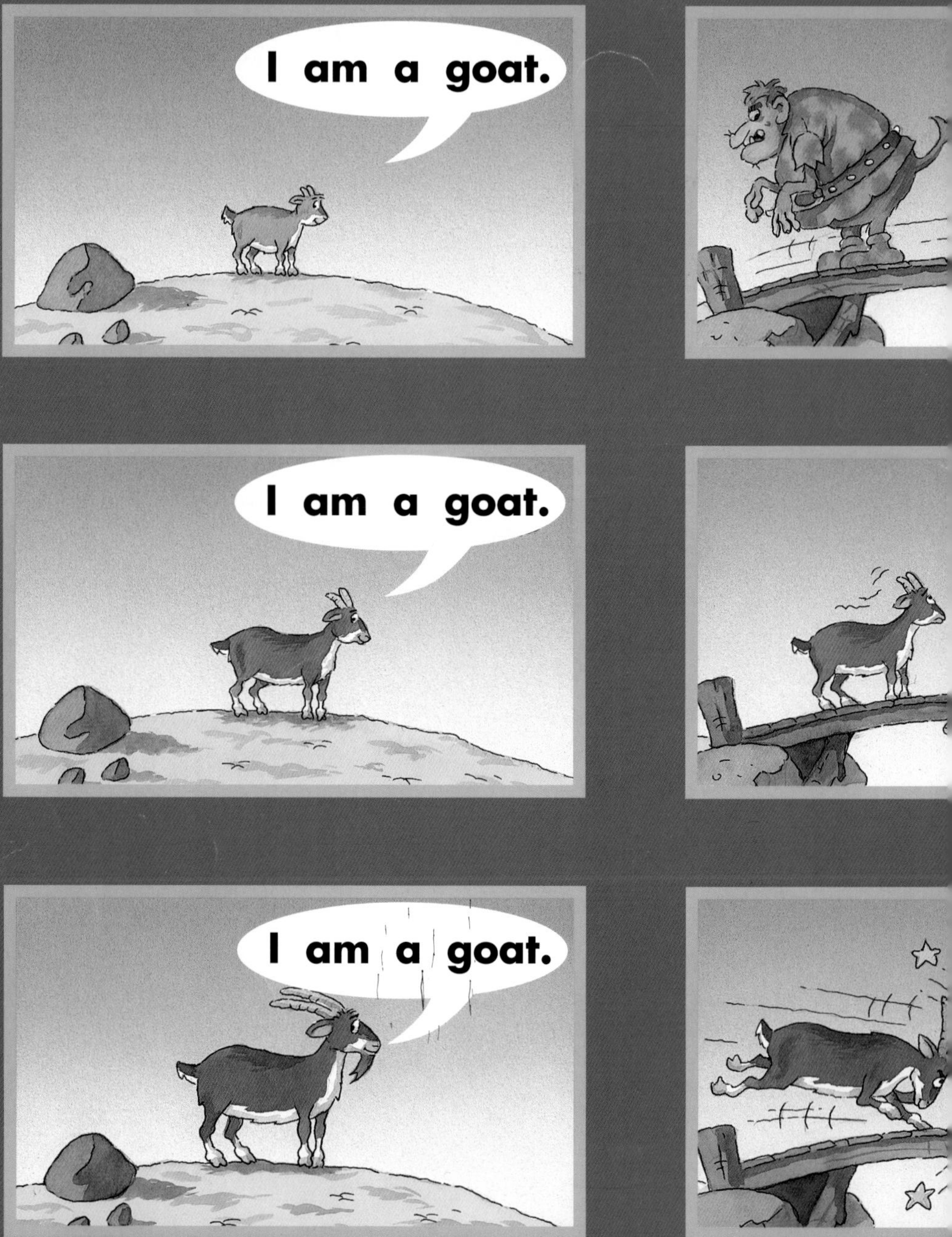
I am a goat.
I am a goat.
I am a goat.

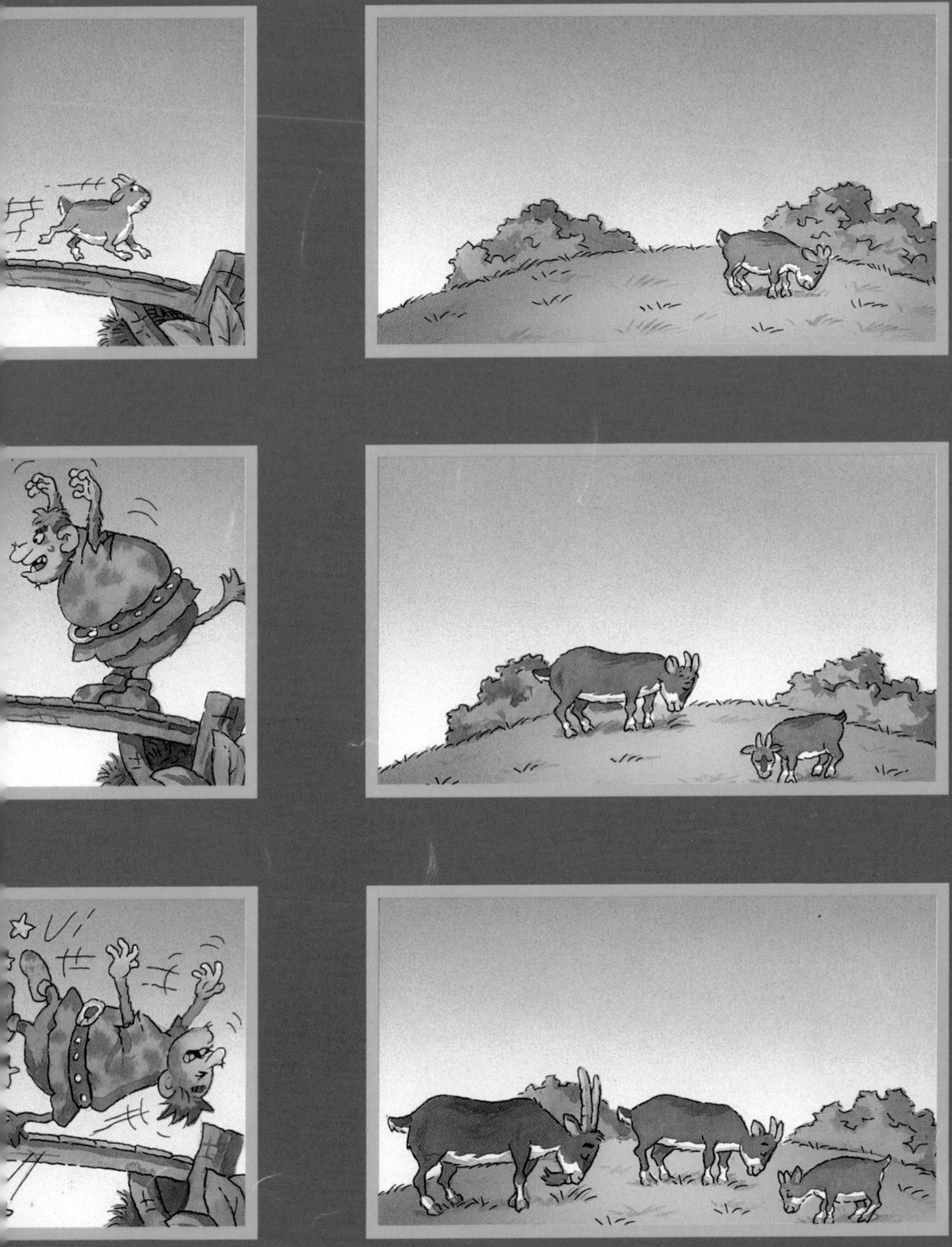

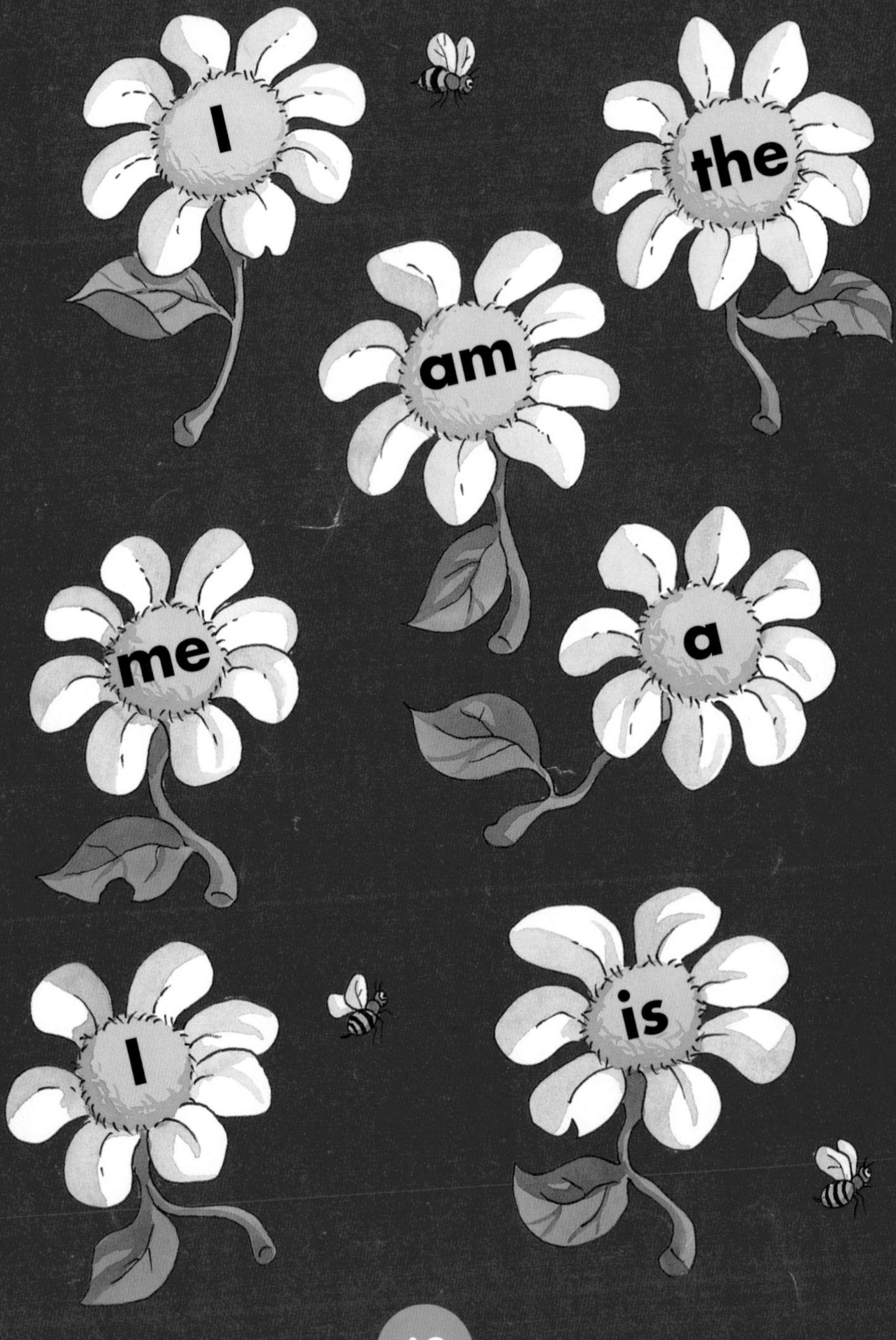
I
the
am
me
a
I
is